O Beautiful
for
Spacious Skies

poem by Katharine Lee Bates

art by Wayne Thiebaud

edited by Sara Jane Boyers

CHRONICLE BOOKS San Francisco

DEDICATION

As always, to Morgan and Lily Kate
and to our assorted dogs, cats, rabbits, lizards, toads, and guppies
who so far haven't eaten the art.

SPECIAL THANKS TO:

Wayne and Betty Jean Thiebaud
The Archives at Wellesley College, Wellesley, Massachusetts
Matt Bult
Paul Thiebaud and Campbell-Thiebaud Gallery, San Francisco, California
Allan Stone Gallery, New York, New York
My agent, Loretta Barrett
My editor, Victoria Rock
— S.J.B.

Katharine Lee Bates photo courtesy of the Archives at Wellesley College, Wellesley, Massachusetts.
Wayne Thiebaud photo courtesy of Matt Bult.
Book design by Laura Lovett.
Typeset in Felt Tip and Graphite.
Printed in Hong Kong.

Library of Congress Cataloging-in-Publication Data
Bates, Katharine Lee, 1859-1929.
O beautiful for spacious skies / poem by Katharine Lee Bates; illustrations by Wayne Thiebaud; edited by Sara Jane Boyers.
32 p.   57 x 69 cm.
Summary: An edition of the nineteenth-century poem that was later set to music, illustrated by a noted American artist.
ISBN 0-8118-0832-7
1. United States—Juvenile poetry. 2. Children's poetry, American. [1. United States—Poetry. 2. American poetry.
3. Songs—United States.] I. Boyers, Sara Jane II. Thiebaud, Wayne, ill. III. Title.
PS1077.B4A8   1994
8119.4—dc20   94-6599   CIP

Distributed in Canada by Raincoast Books
8680 Cambie Street, Vancouver, B.C. V6P 6M9

10 9 8 7 6 5 4 3 2 1

Chronicle Books
275 Fifth Street
San Francisco, California 94103

PREFACE

When I decided to create a series of books pairing the work of contemporary visual artists with evocative poetry, it immediately became clear that the best way to illustrate the wonder of each was to show the magic of their combination. Wayne Thiebaud and Katharine Lee Bates never met. They are of different times, yet each had something to say. Each felt something which, through their work, speaks to the other and echoes feelings we all have. That is the universality of fine art.

Part of what makes great art is that we can find in it something of ourselves. We are not required to love it or even to understand it. But when we stand in front of an image that moves us, or when we read words that bring a cherished memory to life or propel us toward a goal, then we realize that we cannot underestimate the role art and poetry play in our lives! They are direct. They are personal. They speak to us. The words or images of their creators become ours.

So think of this book as a conversation that you and I and the artist and poet each have with ourselves and with one another. And when you are finished with this book, explore art and poetry even further. Some of the museums which have works in their collection by Wayne Thiebaud are listed in the back of this book. But even if your local museum does not possess one of his works, visit it anyway! You might not have known about Wayne Thiebaud before you read this book. There is a good chance you will discover other artists whose work makes you laugh, makes you angry, makes you sad, makes you think. But remember, you need not look only in a museum. Look on the walls of your favorite restaurant. Visit art galleries. Read another book or a magazine. The more you look, the more you will realize that art is everywhere. Simply look.

Poetry, too, is all around us. Since Katharine Lee Bates lived so long ago, few of her works remain in print. However, many of her books are in the library. You might also explore other poets who have written verse so full of imagery that we can illustrate it in our minds. Poems, stories, songs—all of these can fill our imagination with pictures. Simply listen.

And the next time you see a painting, a drawing, or a photograph, think of what words you might want to pair with it. The next time you hear words that bring images to your mind, think about what piece of visual art you might want to pair with them. Perhaps you will want to write some poetry of your own or to paint a painting. Whatever you decide, join the conversation!

Sara Jane Boyers

O BEAUTIFUL
FOR SPACIOUS SKIES,
FOR AMBER WAVES
OF GRAIN,

For purple mountain majesties above the fruited plain!

AMERICA! AMERICA!

GOD SHED HIS GRACE ON THEE

7/25   ♡/ Diebenkorn (1905–
                                                        1990

And crown thy good with brotherhood from sea to shining sea!

O BEAUTIFUL FOR PILGRIM FEET,

WHOSE STERN, IMPASSIONED STRESS

A THOROUGHFARE
FOR FREEDOM BEAT
ACROSS THE
WILDERNESS!

AMERICA! AMERICA!

GOD MEND THINE EVERY FLAW,

CONFIRM THY SOUL IN SELF-CONTROL,

THY LIBERTY IN LAW!

O BEAUTIFUL FOR HEROES PROVED

IN LIBERATING STRIFE,

WHO MORE THAN SELF THEIR COUNTRY LOVED,

AND MERCY MORE THAN LIFE!

AMERICA! AMERICA!

MAY GOD THY GOLD REFINE,

TILL ALL SUCCESS BE NOBLENESS,

AND EVERY GAIN DIVINE!

O BEAUTIFUL FOR PATRIOT DREAM

THAT SEES BEYOND THE YEARS

THINE ALABASTER CITIES GLEAM

UNDIMMED BY HUMAN TEARS!

AMERICA! AMERICA!

GOD SHED HIS GRACE ON THEE

AND CROWN THY GOOD

WITH BROTHERHOOD

FROM SEA TO SHINING SEA!

KATHARINE LEE BATES

Even in her childhood, it was very clear to Katharine Lee Bates that her life was to revolve around writing. Born in 1859 into an old American family (her ancestors journeyed to America on a pilgrim ship in 1635), Bates was inspired and encouraged at a very early age to read, to write, and to learn. She wrote constantly, often ignoring her dolls and other toys except to use them as characters in make-believe stories. When she was nine years old, her mother gave her a diary, establishing Bates's life-long habit of recording thoughts, events, and poetry.

Bates spent her early years in the sailing town of Falmouth, Massachusetts. At the age of twelve, her family moved to Wellesley, Massachusetts, where she was to spend most of her life. By the time she was in high school, her talents as a poet were already recognized and, during her student years at Wellesley College, she sold her first poem for publication to the *Atlantic Monthly*.

Following graduation, Bates taught high school and women's college preparatory classes. In 1886, she was offered an instructorship in English Literature at Wellesley College, where she later advanced to become Chairman of the Department.

At the turn of the century, the early feminist movement was extremely strong and active. Her years at Wellesley provided Bates the opportunity to be at the forefront of educating women for the upcoming century. She was able to shape the college's programs and to offer advice and encouragement to her students. Her door was always open to family, friends, students, and visiting writers.

Bates traveled extensively throughout Europe, spending much time at Oxford, England, doing scholarly research and in Spain, encouraging women's education. And, always, she wrote: stories, poems, essays, and children's poems and stories—thirty-two volumes in all. Her writing was greatly influenced by her travels, her love of nature, her devotion to friends, animals, and children, her passion for social justice, and her great love for her country.

"America the Beautiful" is the embodiment of the ideal America which Katharine Lee Bates envisioned. It was directly inspired by her first trip west in 1893 to spend the summer teaching in Colorado. She traveled by rail, first stopping in Chicago. There, she visited the World's Columbian Exposition, whose featured exhibit was a startling architectural construction of cities of the future—towering buildings nicknamed "the White City." Her cross-country journey continued through the "fertile prairies" of the Midwest, culminating with her teaching duties beneath the "purple ranges of the Rockies." At the end of the summer, she joined her friends for an expedition to the summit of Pike's Peak.

Looking out across the "sea-like expanse of fertile country spreading away so far under those ample skies," the opening lines of the "hymn" (as she referred to the poem) immediately came to her. Jotting them in her ever-present notebook along with several additional stanzas, they were put away for two years, then resurrected and offered for publication. "America the Beautiful" was first published on July 4, 1895. It was subsequently revised in 1904, the final version appearing soon thereafter.

In her exaltation in the beauty of the United States and her desires for its citizens, Katharine Lee Bates wrote what instantly became one of the most popular and familiar works reflecting the hope, passion, and wonder of the nation. Through the years, many put it to music. Although seemingly specific to the United States, many other countries saw within the lyrics hope and strength for their own people, and it was adapted many times, most successfully with "O Canada" and "Mi Méjico". Until the 1930s, when "The Star Spangled Banner" was officially so designated, "America the Beautiful" was considered by many the anthem of the United States. It continues to be the unofficial anthem, its celebration of unity still as powerful as when it was first written.

Katharine Lee Bates died in 1929 at Wellesley. For her time, she led an emancipated life and served as a model for generations of Americans. Through her most famous work, she continues to inspire us today.

Many of Katharine Lee Bates's writings were created for her academic audience. Her writings for children and her poetry collections include the following:

For children:

Fairy Gold. New York, E. P. Dutton and Company, 1916
In Sunny Spain with Pilarica and Rafael. New York, E.P. Dutton and Company, 1913
Little Robin Stay-Behind and Other Plays in Verse for Children. New York, The Woman's Press, 1924
Rose and Thorn. Boston, The Congregational Sunday-School and Publishing Society, 1889
Sunshine and Other Verses. Printed by the Wellesley Alumnae, 1890

For all readers:

America the Beautiful and Other Poems. New York, Thomas Y. Crowell Company, 1911
Selected Poems. Boston, Houghton Mifflin Company, 1930 (published posthumously)
Yellow Clover, A Book of Remembrance. New York, E.P. Dutton and Company, 1922

WAYNE THIEBAUD

Wayne Thiebaud, painter and teacher, directs our vision to his unique view of America. Whether it be decorated cakes aligned in a luscious display or a city with wildly careening streets, he chronicles for us those objects and landscapes of our lives which are overlooked and taken for granted, but whose time, style, and manner are telltale signs of who we are.

Born in Mesa, Arizona, in 1920, but raised primarily in Southern California, Wayne Thiebaud developed an early interest in cartooning, drawing, and set design. He first sought work as an illustrator in high school, working at Walt Disney Studios as an animator for Jiminy Cricket, Goofy, and Pinocchio cartoons. In 1941, he joined the United States Army Air Force as a cartoonist and illustrator, and continued working as a cartoonist and commercial artist following World War II.

In the late 1940s, he returned to college as an art major, graduating from California State College, Sacramento in 1951. In the 1950s, he began his distinguished parallel career as a college art professor, first at Sacramento Junior College (ultimately becoming Chairman of the Art Department) and, from the 1960s on, at the University of California at Davis.

Early in his artistic career, Thiebaud began to introduce into his art objects remembered from his youth—the foods and glass counter displays of his childhood on the ocean boardwalk of Long Beach, California. Frosted, packaged, and displayed, his subjects have been "transformed," dressed up and made to look special, and he paints them as a comment upon our need to present ourselves as more than we are.

Thiebaud exhibited first in California. Determined that his work be seen, he even hung his paintings in restaurants, furniture stores, and drive-in movie snack bars. Critics initially received his work with some skepticism—one critic, referring to the many images of food, called him "the hungriest artist in California." But in

1962, he showed with great success at a New York gallery, and his work became well known.

In 1963, Thiebaud expanded his work to figure paintings, believing that the figure is the key to perfecting drawing. Whereas the still lifes were drawn from memory, the figures were often drawn in studio settings. Landscapes were added to the artist's repertoire in 1966, and in the 1970s, cityscapes.

Thiebaud's art has had many influences, among them many nineteenth century French and Italian realists, including Courbet, Manet, Degas, and the Italian I Macchiaioli school; Edward Hopper; the brash and bold Abstract Expressionists; and the San Francisco Bay Area painters who incorporated elements of abstraction into their own representational painting, along with a distinct color palette.

In the work of Wayne Thiebaud, the presence of the painter is always evident in his strong handling of the medium. Approaching pies, candied apples, lipsticks, toys, human figures, and city streets, he is interested in the artist's traditional investigation into form, color, shape, and the effect of light. This can be seen in the way he isolates a subject, often surrounding it with an intense color line; the way he dramatically tips the horizon line; and in the humor of his characterization. The objects often have an emotional and symbolic meaning, and he renders them in truly delectable glory (icing painted so richly one feels able to lick it off the surface).

Working in almost every medium, including oil, acrylic, and watercolor, as well as printmaking, Wayne Thiebaud examines and re-examines his work, reworking ideas and images he approached as early as the 1950s. Each examination incorporates new learning devices, new risks. Constantly honing his skills, he has attended life drawing classes weekly for over forty years, and he carries with him a notebook, always sketching—at home, in a lecture hall, on an airplane. He is not afraid to acknowledge failure—a factor he considers an "essential part of the creative process."

Thiebaud's work is represented in many important museum collections throughout the world. He has been honored many times as both a distinguished artist and teacher, and has been commissioned for various public projects.

Many artists have painted the American scene, but few have given it the full examination and contemporary slant of Wayne Thiebaud, a realist who has learned to combine the best elements of perception, memory, and abstraction. An artist who readily acknowledges his inspiration by others, he stands independent of any one movement. Art, he maintains, is a continuing investigation, drawing upon memory and history to be combined with issues and skills learned just today to continually bring visual excitement and surprise, approximating real life.

Wayne Thiebaud's work can be found in collections around the world, including the following museums:

Museum of Modern Art, New York, New York
Whitney Museum of American Art, New York, New York
San Francisco Museum of Modern Art, San Francisco, California
The Metropolitan Museum of Art, New York, New York
Philadelphia Museum of Art, Philadelphia, Pennsylvania
The Corcoran Gallery of Art , Washington, DC
Albright-Knox Art Gallery, Buffalo, New York
National Gallery of Art, Washington, DC
The Nelson-Atkins Museum of Art, Kansas City, Missouri
The Tate Gallery, London, England
Victoria and Albert Museum, London, England

ART CREDITS